Where Is God?

The Little Angel Books Series

Where Is God?

Written & Illustrated

by Leia A. Stinnett

Cover art by Leia Stinnett

ISBN 0-929385-90-X

Published by
StarChild Press
a division of
Light Technology
Publishing
P.O. Box 1526
Sedona, Arizona 86339
(520) 282-6523

Printed by
MISSION POSSIBLE
Commercial
Printing

P.O. Box 1495
Sedona, AZ 86339

John was a very loving, inquisitive boy with large brown eyes that seemed to twinkle as he spoke and light brown hair that flopped over one eyebrow, partially hiding his right eye from the world.

John liked to investigate things. He liked to take things apart to see how they were made. He loved to read about different parts of God's beautiful world, about people and how they lived, and about plants, animals and insects. He wanted to know about everything.

He especially enjoyed looking at and studying the stars in the deep night sky.

He would place a blanket on the lawn in his backyard and gaze up at the glittering stars for hours.

There would always be one twinkling star in particular that he would single out, one very bright star that seemed to wink at him.

While watching this star, John would wonder, "Who is God? Where is God?"

For as long as John could remember, he had a warm, loving feeling every time he thought about God. But whenever he asked someone, "Who is God?" or "Where is God?" no one could give him an answer that felt right to him.

He had, in fact, received so many different answers to what he felt was a very simple question deserving a very simple answer, that John became more and more confused, and more and more determined to find out just who

God was, where He was, and why God was always hiding from everyone.

When John and his parents first moved into their new home, they visited different churches each Sunday, looking for the one church in which they felt the most comfortable.

This search gave John the opportunity to listen to how different people felt about God.

Each Sunday John dressed in his dark blue suit, white shirt and red and white bow tie. He was excited as he polished his shiny black shoes, anticipating that on this day he would find out the truth about God.

In visiting many churches, John was able to learn just how different they were from each other. He noted that some were very small with very plain furnishings, nothing fancy.

Others, he discovered, were very large and very ornate with beautiful

GOD = GOOD
HELL = BAD
?
?
?
?

stained-glass windows and beautiful religious statues of holy figures, Jesus and angels.

As he looked at the structure of each, he realized they all felt different, but they all had one thing in common – they were all considered God's house.

John felt peace, he felt love and he felt very protected, but he just wasn't sure about God living in these buildings.

John also reflected on the messages offered by the different ministers of the churches he had visited.

He realized most of the messages seemed to make him feel God was very separate from His people, from His children. The messages seemed to depict God as a very loving Father, watching over the children of Earth, rewarding them for following His rules and punishing them when they disobeyed.

John remembered hearing the words of a very old minister in one of the oldest churches in town, words which brought cold chills to his spine.

The minister took this punishment thing a step further by describing hell as a place people were sent after they died if they disobeyed God's laws.

"How could a loving Father send His children to such an awful place?" John wondered. "Was God truly someone to fear?"

So here John was, in still another church, sitting in the pew, wiggling and squirming, trying to get comfortable. Even though the seat was very hard and very uncomfortable, John had made up his mind that today he would get the answers he was looking for.

"Today, I will find out who God is and where God lives; I just know it," said John with a look of determination on his face.

John rested his head back on the pew and closed his eyes.

He let his mind take him to a very special place inside himself where he imagined himself as being a soft pink cloud, drifting up toward the heavens, higher, higher . . . higher.

As he envisioned himself as a cloud, high in the sky, John could faintly hear Rev. Smyth's words.

Suddenly, John snapped back into full awareness of what Rev. Smyth was saying.

Rev. Smyth was talking about God's laws, the Ten Commandments. He was describing how we need to follow God's laws to assure our place in heaven.

The tone of Rev. Smyth's voice changed as he began talking about people's "sins."

What is a sin? John wondered, his eyes drawn into an intense frown.

Rev. Smyth described the breaking of God's laws as sinning. He went on to describe God as a forgiving God; however, people who sinned had to pray to God for forgiveness and promise never to sin again. Rev. Smyth added that if a person continued to sin, he/she would be punished.

Sounded just like the way things worked at home, John thought. When he disobeyed his parents, he was punished – a privilege was taken away or he was not allowed to do something he really wanted to do.

When he did what he was asked to do, when he obeyed his parents, he was rewarded with privileges and with the things he wanted to do.

It all seemed so final. There was good over on this side and bad over there. If you are good, you are rewarded, and if you are bad, you are punished. Something still wasn't right with this picture, John rationalized.

Because John was inquisitive, because John wanted to know the facts about everything, John had great difficulty in accepting much of the words he had heard in the churches he had visited to this point. In fact, he felt confused.

He realized church was a very special place where people could gather and share in a loving, spiritual environment, learning about God, what God wanted them to know about Him, what He would share with them and what He would give to them.

He felt churches were very important to help people understand their connection to God and how God could help them live a happier life, but something was missing. Something wasn't clear.

Not one minister told him what he wanted to hear. Where was God?

Who was God? Why didn't anyone really know?

As John sat at the breakfast table, he looked over at his mother. In a soft, quiet voice he asked, "Mom, who is God? Where does God live? Why can't I see Him? Why can't I find Him?"

His mother turned and looked at John with an intense look of astonishment.

"John . . . why John! You know very well who God is. Haven't you been listening to all the messages in church each Sunday? Haven't you been studying your Sunday school lessons? Why do you ask so many questions?"

John realized how difficult it was for his mother to try to explain answers to his questions. What he realized was that she truly did not know who God is or where to find

Him herself . . . not really!

She tried to explain to John in much the same way as had the ministers of some of the more recent church visits. What she described tended to separate God from John and the people of Earth; a God who could not be seen or felt in a physical sense by any people on Earth.

John experienced this strange, gnawing sensation in the pit of his stomach, the feeling that always told him when something was not quite right. Something was wrong with Mother's story. Something was not quite right with the pictures painted by the church ministers, and John was going to find out the truth!

As John walked to school, he looked up at the crystal blue sky dotted with a few white fluffy clouds. The stars were up there . . . somewhere. God was up there . . .

somewhere. Somewhere! John just knew it, but where?

Why couldn't he find an answer to his question? What was the big secret?

It was always so easy to get answers to his questions from his parents, friends and teachers, and from the books that he read, in which there were answers to every question, except about God.

John began to walk a bit faster. He didn't want to be late for school.

As he walked, he breathed in the world around him – the trees, the fragrances of the flowers, the fresh air, the songs of the birds and the buzzing of the bees.

He began to imagine the last trip his family took to Bear Lake.

He remembered the beautiful snow-capped mountains.

He remembered the crystal clear

lake, the fresh scent of the pine trees.

And he remembered the gentleness of the timid deer that came into camp searching for apples.

It was beautiful. God's world was truly beautiful!

John knew that God had created all these beautiful things for people to enjoy.

Yet . . . if God created all this beauty to make us comfortable and happy, how could He turn around and make such a horrible place as hell?

How could He be so cold and harsh?

How could He send people to such a horrible place after they died?

People make mistakes. Maybe sins are just mistakes . . . things we have to learn on this Earth?

Hmmm! John had to think about all of this.

"No one deserves such a fate,"

HISTORY

said John, his face wrinkled in disgust. "No one, no matter what he/she does here on Earth, deserves to be punished in such a way!"

At school John decided to ask his friend Freddie what he thought about God.

Freddie thought for a short time and then responded. "Well, I always thought God was this very old man. You know, like the old man that you see on New Year's Eve – the old year guy – Father Time?

"You know, the guy with the long, white beard carrying that funny looking stick with the curved thing on the end?

"Oh, yeah! And God has this thing He carries in His other hand, too . . . like a lightning bolt!

"He sits in this big, gold chair like a king has and throws these bolts at people who are bad. I hear He can really hit His targets, too. At least that's what my dad tells me.

"God can send hurricanes and floods and stuff to hurt people, my dad says."

Freddie went on a bit longer to describe hell as though he had actually been there himself.

But the words just didn't seem right to John. "This couldn't possibly be God who Freddie was talking about. No, something was wrong here," John said to himself.

On the way home from school, John stopped to talk to his neighbor, Mr. Johnston.

"Mr. Johnston, I've got a question for you . . . a very important question. Who is God? Where does God live?" John hoped for a quick and appropriate response to his question, one he could accept.

"Why, John, there's no such person.

MATH

There is no God," Mr. Johnston said rather callously.

"Do you want to know why I say that? Want to know how I know that?" Mr. Johnson added gruffly.

John slowly shook his head up and down to acknowledge that he did in fact want to know why he had said that.

John looked a bit shocked at Mr. Johnson's reply.

"For your information, if there really was a God, my boy," Mr. Johnston continued, "I would have gotten all those things I asked for a long time ago – lots of money, a new car, not having to work so hard to make a living, a vacation around the world.

"And I begged God not to let Mildred, my wife, suffer and die, but you know what? He didn't hear a word I said . . . or maybe He just didn't care about us!

"No, there is no such person as God!" Mr. Johnston's comment was final.

John was very troubled by Mr. Johnston's words.

"No God? Oh, no! Mr. Johnston, you are very wrong. I will find a way to show you there really is a God. I will show you. I will find out who God really is! Then I will show you!" John was beginning to cry as these words left his lips.

John ran into his house, up the stairs to his room and dropped his books on his bed. Without stopping for a breath or a bite to eat, John dashed down the stairs and out the back door, out into the yard.

He found a secluded place to sit in the warm Sun under the old oak tree. He sat on the ground, leaning hard with his back against the tree's sturdy trunk.

John removed his shoes and buried his feet in the tall grass. For a short time, John held his face in his hands and sobbed quietly.

As he opened his eyes, he let his gaze move upward, straining to see the face of God in the bright blue sky.

"God, who are you? Please show me!

"Where can I find you?

"Everyone I have talked to has told me things about you that I know are not true. I want to know the truth! I want to hear it from you!" John demanded.

John let his eyes close, allowing his thoughts to travel upward . . . higher . . . higher . . . until he felt he was touching the clouds up to where he remembered the little star twinkling in the night sky.

Higher and higher John took his imagination. Higher and higher until he was floating out into the universe,

away from the Earth, out past the stars and planets.

The stars and planets passed by his imagination. The Sun and Moon moved by as well, but he didn't see God.

John opened his eyes and held his face in his hands. He began to sob, whimpering to himself, "Why doesn't God show Himself? What is the big secret, anyway?

"Maybe Rev. Smyth was right. Maybe Mom and Freddie were right. Maybe Mr. Johnston was right after all. Maybe God doesn't want to let me see Him, or maybe there is no such person as God."

Suddenly, John felt a powerful but very loving energy surround his whole body. He felt very much at peace, very much a part of the world around him. In fact, he felt as though he were a part of the whole universe.

God spoke to John through John's thoughts and feelings.

"John, you know me. You have always known me. I am inside of you. I am inside and outside of all things. We are all one family. I am a part of you. You are a part of me.

"I was lonely out here in the universe, so I created the Earth. Then I created the plants and trees, the oceans, rivers, lakes and streams. I created the animals and birds, the beautiful flowers. I even created the little insects.

"Then I created boys and girls just like you. I created all these things from a part of me, from my own energy. Your soul – your real body – is energy that is always a part of me.

"I am everywhere. With my energy, I can be a part of everything. I can see everything that goes on in the whole universe. I know everything.

"Because you are now and will

GOD
AND
I

always be a part of me, you have my energy available to use in healing yourself, in finding answers to problems that occur in your life, in knowing anything you need to know to make your life happier and more loving. If you ask for my help, I will most assuredly give it to you lovingly.

"To know who I am, simply know yourself. Go inside and feel the truly loving, spiritual being that you are.

"To know me, you must give of yourself, be willing to help other people, the Earth's creatures, the Earth herself.

"To know me is to live in peace and harmony and to help bring peace, joy and love to the Earth in all that you do.

"I am love. To know love is to know me."

God continued speaking through John's thoughts.

"You have come to Earth to learn

lessons. There is no right or wrong, only lessons. If you do something that is not loving and kind, that you don't feel right about doing, you will know it is not right for you. You will learn what is right for you from experiences, from the things that you do that make you feel good.

"You learn what makes you happy. You learn what makes you unhappy. You can change things that make you unhappy, just by changing the way you think and act. Loving, positive, happy thoughts create a loving, positive, happy life for you.

"Remember . . . no matter what you choose to do, I will always be with you. I will always love you. I am a part of you and you are a part of me. Where I go, you go. Where you go, I go."

John knew immediately that God was warm, loving and kind.

John could feel the energy. He realized that God was truly a part of

all that He/She had created – the stars, plants, Earth, clouds, trees, plants, flowers, animals, birds and insects. All the people of the Earth, no matter what color their skin, where they live, or what they believe, they are all part of God, and God loves them all equally. Just as God loves me, thought John.

John knew that God did not punish anyone. He felt people sort of punished themselves in learning their lessons.

If they did something in their life that did not make them happy, they learned what not to do the next time the same situation occurred.

John knew that if people would make changes in their lives – positive loving changes, bringing in more love, joy and happiness – they would find life full of wonderful experiences that they could share with the world.

John also learned that hell was something created by people's fears. He felt that God had expressed to him that He/She was truly love, joy and harmony; that humankind created their own kind of hell by letting their feelings control them feelings of hate, anger, selfishness, greed and the like.

These thoughts satisfied John on this subject. He felt very relieved.

John could hardly wait to tell everyone about his experience.

He ran to tell his mother first.

She was a bit emotional and seemed somewhat relieved when John told her about God's visit in the backyard. To John's amazement, she did not question his story at all, but seemed to absorb every word, as something she had been wanting to hear for a very long time.

John called Freddie on the telephone and proudly relayed to his

friend what he had just experienced.

Freddie replied, "Wow! I'll have to think about that one.

"Maybe if I stop worrying about being punished by God for everything all the time, I'll be a lot happier, too."

Then John ran next door to Mr. Johnston's house.

"Mr. Johnston, Mr. Johnston . . . I found God, and He/She wants to talk to you, too! God has something very special to say to you!"

John's story brought Mr. Johnston close to tears. John talked to him about how God loves all of us equally, how He/She would help us if we would only work harder to help ourselves be more loving and kind. He told Mr. Johnston how God lives inside each of us equally, no matter what color we are, what we believe, or what kind of a person we think we are – good or bad.

John went on to tell Mr. Johnston that God lived inside even those people who really did not believe God was real.

"God doesn't punish us, Mr. Johnston. God helps us by letting us learn our own lessons. We can make our lives happy and loving, or we can be unhappy – it's our choice.

"God always loves us, no matter what we think or feel about ourselves, no matter whether we feel loving and kind or angry, God still loves us. You sure can't say that about a lot of people here on Earth, even some of your friends."

Mr. Johnston had tears in his eyes while John continued to talk to him about the experience he had just had with God.

The old man realized that he had been blaming God for all the things that he had created in his own life. He realized how much his wife had been suffering, and God had taken her to live with Him/Her, so she wouldn't have to suffer any longer.

Mr. Johnston reached down and pulled John to him, holding him very close for a long time. John's words had truly touched his heart.

Mr. Johnston remembered he had lost the feeling of love a long time ago and just never bothered looking for love again.

John's experience had brought back love to his heart. A warm glow filled Mr. Johnston, and a loving smile beamed across his face as he waved good-bye to John.

John related his experience to his Sunday school class the following weekend.

Then John led the children outside of the church classroom,

under a row of old oak trees.

John asked them to sit on the lawn with their backs against the trees. Then he described his experience with God coming to visit him.

He asked them to close their eyes, and he would help them visit with God, too.

"God will speak to you, too.

"Are you ready to go inside yourself to find God?"

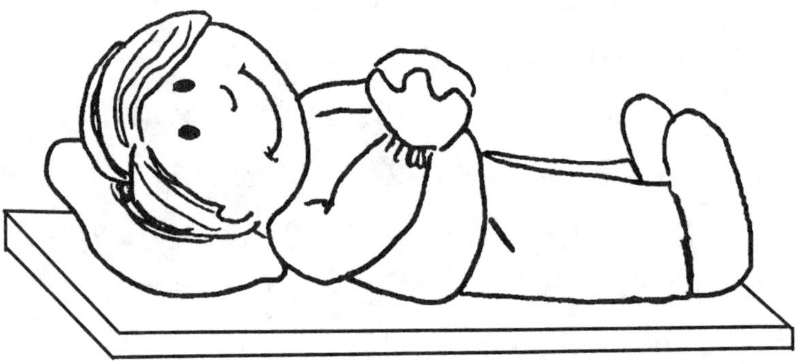

MEDITATION

Take a few nice deep breaths, as you get into a very relaxed position, either lying down or sitting in a chair with your spine very straight.

Breathe in and out. Count evenly as you breathe. Breathe in to the count of eight and breathe out to the count of eight.

Breathe from the bottom of your abdomen all the way up to the top of your head, and then breathe down and out. Keep breathing this way for about ten breaths.

Now take your attention all the way down to your toes and imagine your toes are relaxing completely.

Bring your attention up into your feet, and imagine your feet are relaxing.

Bring your attention into your ankles and heels, and imagine your ankles and heels are relaxing.

Move your attention into the calves of

your legs, and imagine they are very relaxed.

Bring your attention into your knees, and let your knees relax.

Move your imagination into your thighs, and let your thighs relax.

Bring your attention into your hips, the tip of your spine, and around to the front of your body in your abdomen, and let all of this area relax completely.

Now bring your attention into your stomach area and your middle back, letting all of this area relax completely.

Bring your attention up into your chest, your lungs and all the way up to the top of your shoulders, and let all of your chest, lungs and shoulders relax completely.

Take your attention into your upper arms, elbows, forearms, wrists, hands, fingers and thumbs, and let your arms and hands relax completely.

Now take your attention from your

fingertips and the tips of your thumbs, and bring it back up to your forearms, elbows and upper arms, all the way up to the top of your shoulders, letting all of this area be totally relaxed.

Bring your relaxing energy up into your neck. Let all the muscles in your neck relax completely.

Draw the relaxing energy up into your face and head, letting all of the muscles in your face and head be completely relaxed.

Now you are completely relaxed and ready to move up into the clouds.

Imagine you are going higher and higher, up higher and higher, floating upward, higher . . . higher . . . higher.

You are moving past the Earth, past the clouds and out into the universe.

You can see stars, planets, and the Moon and Sun. You can float in the universe, and you are safe and protected in God's pure white light as you travel.

Imagine you are surrounded by a warm, loving energy, a very powerful but loving energy.

You feel very comfortable. You feel very loved. You feel as though you are connected very closely to this energy.

Now focus all your attention deep within yourself at your center, your solar plexus.

Let your mind and body be very quiet. Be as still and as quiet as you can.

Keep your eyes closed and concentrate very hard on your center. Nothing outside of yourself . . . just your center.

Imagine a beautiful light in your center – a yellow, purple, blue or white light – whatever color you like best.

Imagine the light becoming very, very large and very, very bright. Concentrate on the feeling of this light growing and becoming brighter within you.

As the light becomes larger and larger, how do you feel in your body?

Are you feeling more and more energy inside of you?

Do you feel very calm and peaceful?

Do you feel more loving and kind toward yourself and others?

Let the light fill your center, then your whole body. Be filled with the light, the love and the peace of God.

Now concentrate all of your energy at your mind's eye, that spot in the center of your forehead between your eyebrows. Stare right at the back of your eyes, at your third-eye center.

Imagine a beautiful blue light growing brighter and brighter, larger and larger. Let the light expand until you begin to see a picture in your mind, a picture of God. God will appear in different ways to different people, or just as a warm, loving feeling.

Listen very carefully to God as He/She speaks to you. If you want to ask a question or receive help with a problem, ask God with your mind for assistance.

Listen very, very carefully, as quietly as you can. A small, quiet, loving voice will speak to you as a sound, a knowing, or a feeling or thought. Wait patiently for the answer.

If you do not hear, feel or know the answer, do not be upset or think you did something wrong. Keep trying.

Do this meditation over and over. Practice!

Very soon you will hear God speak to you.

Now let your eyes open very slowly and come back into awareness of the room around you.

Do you feel more loving and peaceful?

Do you feel happier?

Do you feel closer to God and all of God's universe?

If you like, draw a picture of God as you saw Him/Her or as you feel He/She looks.

What God Looks Like to Me:

Other Books by Leia Stinnett:

A Circle of Angels
The Twelve Universal Laws

The Little Angel Books Series:
The Angel Told Me to Tell You Good-bye
The Bridge Between Two Worlds
Color Me One
Crystals R for Kids
Exploring the Chakras
Happy Feet
One Red Rose
When the Earth Was New
Who's Afraid of the Dark?

All My Angel Friends (Coloring Book)

About the Author

The '80s were a decade of self-discovery for Leia Stinnett after she began researching many different avenues of spirituality. In her profession as a graphic designer she had become restless, knowing there was something important she had to do outside the materiality of corporate America.

In August 1986 Leia had her first contact with Archangel Michael when he appeared in a physical form of glowing blue light. A voice said, "I am Michael. Together we will save the children."

In 1988 she was inspired by Michael to teach spiritual classes in Sacramento, California, the Circle of Angels. Through these classes she had the opportunity to work with learning-disabled children, children of abuse and those from dysfunctional homes.

Later Michael told her, "Together we are going to write the Little Angel Books." To date Leia and Michael have created thirteen Little Angel Books that present various topics of spiritual truths and principles. The books proved popular among adults as well as children.

The Circle of Angels classes have been introduced to several countries around the world and across the U.S., and Leia and her husband Douglas now have a teacher's manual and training program for people who wish to offer spiritual classes to children. Leia and Michael have been interviewed on Canadian Satellite TV and have appeared on NBC-TV's *Angels II – Beyond the Light*, which featured their Circle of Angels class and discussed their books and Michael's visit.

The angels have given Leia and Douglas a vision of a new educational system without competition or grades — one that supports love and positive self-esteem, honoring all children as the independent lights they are. Thus they are now writing a curriculum for the new "schools of light" and developing additional books and programs for children.